NOW THAT I'VE MET THE REAL YOU

By

Joseph Nixon

Contents

THE STORY 5

    CHAPTER 1 5

    CHAPTER 2 17

    CHAPTER 3 27

    CHAPTER 4 33

    CHAPTER 5 45

    CHAPTER 6 55

    CHAPTER 7 69

    CHAPTER 8 77

THE DISCUSSION 89

    INTRODUCTION...91

    MEETING THE REPRESENTATIVE 95

    THE CHASE 103

    PILLOW TALK 111

    SHACKING UP... 115

    HELLO STRANGER.......................................123

    NOW THAT I'VE MET

    THE REAL YOU! 129

    ENDORSEMENTS 135

Joseph Nixon

CHAPTER 1

THE STORY

It's now 8:30 pm, Jay beams with contentment as he sinks comfortingly into his leather executive chair, spinning aimlessly from right to left. He just helped Johnson Construction, a Fortune 500 company acquire Southeastern Construction. As Jay cleans off his desk, he zeroes in on the frustrated yet incredibly intelligent analysts and associates on his team, most of whom had been in the office since 5:45 am. Strung out from coffee, their faces tell the story of a long day! Jay can empathize with caffeine binges intended to promote productivity that only lead to more frustration and a lack of productivity.

"Goodnight, guys," exclaims Jay as he loosens the perfect dimple in his necktie and prepares to leave the office. Then, he murmurs to himself, "It's celebration time!" He rubs his hands together back and forth as he enters the elevator, pondering the big commission in his future. As Jay is staring through the opaque glass elevator, his thoughts are equally unclear on where he would celebrate such a momentous occasion. Ding cries the elevator as it finally descends upon the ground floor of the twenty-five-story building.

Jay anxiously exits the elevator on his way to commemorate his latest achievement. The thing is, he has no idea where this celebration will take place. Jay sends a text message to his best friend, Tim.

Jay: Hey, brother, guess what?

Tim: You got us front row tickets to the basketball game!

Jay: No, better than that.

Tim: You ran into that bikini model we've been talking about!

Jay: No, fool, better than that! I just closed another huge deal!

Tim: I don't know if that's better than the bikini model, but that's great! So, do I meet you at V.I.P. in the VIP?

Jay: Humph – I'm not sure. This deal is different. It moves me closer to my goal. I want the celebration to be different this time. I'll probably know where I'm going once I get there. Whatever I decide, I'll call you.

Tim: Alright, just let me know.

As Jay walks into Exquisite, an upscale jazz club in the heart of the city, the music is playing softly as a whisper in the background. The subdued lighting dims the room with a luminous light peeking behind the top shelf bottles, adorning the shelves at the bar. As Jay surveys the room, he notices an attractive woman alone at the end of the bar. Feeling euphoric about his day, Jay approaches.

"Hi, beautiful, how are you this evening?"

The young lady places her silver clutch purse on the bar,

and with a raised brow looks up and replies, "I'm great, thanks for asking."

"My name is Jay and yours?"

With a blissful look on her face, she replies, "My name is Chantell."

"May I join you for a drink?," Jay asks cheekily.

Chantell hesitates before she responds, looks around at the opulent setting surrounding the bar and with a smirk, replies, "I suppose, considering the bar doesn't belong to me."

"Do I hear a little sarcasm in your voice?" Asks Jay as he carefully extracts the deeply-cushioned, leather bar stool.

Chantell smiles without saying a word. Her face is oval shaped with high prominent cheekbones. Her teeth are pearly white, her lips luscious and her hazel eyes are mesmerizing giving off the "Puss in Boots" effect.

Snapping out of his temporary hypnotic state, Jay asks, "May I buy you a drink?"

Chantell slides her unfinished plate of hors-d'oeuvres to the side and says, "I'm not supposed to accept gifts from a stranger."

With a crooked smirk on his face, Jay makes another offer to buy Chantell a drink.

Chantell turns and faces Jay. "I see you're pretty persistent, and I hate to impose, but since you insist," replies Chantell.

With his hand raised, Jay leans over the marble-top bar and makes eye contact with the bartender. His striking black and chrome wristwatch glistens with the slightest of light.

As the bartender approaches, Jay says to him, "Give this beautiful young lady whatever she would like to drink."

Chantell leans back slightly on her backless bar stool with her neck slightly tilted. She has an inscrutable look on her face.

Jay's forehead furrows. What did I say? Jay thinks to himself.

Chantell then replies, "Beautiful and young, I don't know much about you Jay, but you seem pretty smart!"

The bartender who has made his way over at Jay's request is wearing black slacks, a white shirt with rolled-up sleeves, a black silk vest, and a black bow tie. He smiles at Chantell's response as he turns to take her order.

"Excuse me," the bartender says, "What would you like to drink?"

"I would like a glass of Moscato."

"And I'll take a double shot of Patron chilled," responds Jay.

Initially, Chantell and Jay are a bit apprehensive. The conversation was minimal, and the awkwardness of meeting someone for the first time had taken over. Luckily, that only lasted for a short while because after Jay's second glass; he becomes more comfortable and talkative.

Sliding his empty, salt-rimmed glass to the side, Jay turns toward Chantell and says, "This place is much nicer than I had anticipated. How often do you hang out here?"

"I've been here a few times. The ambiance is nice here,and it's a good place to relax after a long day's work. Especially for me because I don't get an opportunity to get out that often,"replies Chantell.

"So, what do you do for a living that keeps you so busy?"

Without hesitation, Chantell responds, "I'm a real estate agent and you?"

"I work for an investment bank here in the city."

"With a quizzical look on her face, Chantel replies, "Investment banking in Atlanta –humph. That's pretty interesting."

"Yes, I know. I get that all the time. Atlanta is not synonymous with investment banking. People think more of New York– you know– Wall Street. Believe it or not, our office competes well with our New York headquarters. We focus on mergers and acquisitions. We look for deals around two hundred and fifty million to the four hundred-million-dollar range."

"Well, that seems impressive! What do you do there?" With a Cheshire cat smile draped across his face, Jay responds, "I'm a Vice President at the bank!"

"Well, excuse me,Mr. Banker!" Exclaims Chantell while laughing and sipping her Moscato slowly.

"What's funny?" Jay asks.

"Nothing, besides the fact that the bass in your voice got deeper as you uttered Vice President!"

Jay chuckles and replies, "You're not only attractive, but you're funny too."

"It's interesting you say that," replies Chantell. "I usually carry the moniker of Ms. Too Serious, but I always thought that I could be pretty funny at times."

"Maybe you haven't met the right person that would make you comfortable enough to be your funny self."

"We've only known each other for about thirty minutes now. So, are you suggesting that I should be comfortable and that you're the right person?"

"I think both," replies Jay.

"You seem to have a way with words. Is that how you close your deals,Mr. Banker, you know, by using slick talk?"

"Slick talk," replies Jay. "I'm not sure why you think I'm engaging in slick talk, but as for my deals, I close those because I'm able to articulate the benefits to my clients in a very succinct manner."Jay sits upright on his barstool with a huge smirk on his face.

They both laugh.

A few hours have passed, and Jay and Chantell continue to become more acquainted. Chantell finishes her second drink.

"Aren't you going to have one more with me?" Jay asks.

"I'm not much of a drinker, and besides, I'll settle for the one to two drink ratio we established here tonight."

"There you go again," replies Jay as he tilts his head back to finish his last drink.

Jay notices the vigor that Chantell exhibited earlier in the evening was waning. He knows that the night with her is about to be over soon. He takes another look at Chantell, who is wearing a red V-neck, draped, hip-hugging, cocktail dress with crystal-embellished platform pumps. Jay couldn't seem to stop his imagination from running wild. Wow, he thought to himself. She's gorgeous. Man, what I would do. No, no, she doesn't look like the type. I better be respectful.

As Jay turns his head slowly, he notices Chantell gawking at him out of the corner of her eye. Jay is wearing a black, slim fit designer suit, with black tassel loafers. Jay is attractive, athletically built and charming.

After wrestling with their thoughts, Chantell and Jay thank each other for an enjoyable time and exchange numbers.

"Call me some time," Jay says as he extends his right hand towards Chantell to help her from her seat. "Would you mind if I ushered you to the front of the club?"

"I don't mind at all, as a matter of fact, you'll be the best-dressed bodyguard in here tonight."

Smirking, Jay then replies, "Well, after you."

Jay and Chantell head for the front door. Chantell's walk is classy. It resembles the walk of a runway model but a little less exaggerated. Chantell and Jay both hand their tickets to the valet and await their cars. Jay is taken aback when he sees this white Lamborghini pull up. As the driver side door wing flies open, Jay notices the custom sexy pink leather interior. He thinks to himself, if she wasn't gorgeous before, her car sure is! Chantell takes one more look at Jay in her rear-view mirror as her car roars away.

Jay is waving goodbye as his rare, metallic gray Bentley Continental GT pulls up. In his George Jefferson strut, Jay ostentatiously slaps a big tip in the hand of the valet as he whistles away, mumbling to himself, "there's nothing better than being equally yoked!"

CHAPTER 2

The next day, Jay is preparing to meet Tim for lunch. Tim is the CEO of Seymour Behavioral, the largest behavioral healthcare conglomerate in the nation. Tim is also the proud father of three beautiful girls and has recently endured a nasty divorce and custody battle. Tim has lost faith in relationships. He believes that his ex-wife made a one hundred and eighty-degree turn as soon as they both said I do.

As Jay approaches Carolina's Deli, he notices Tim sitting in his customary seat as he gazes through the deli window from a distance. Carolina's Deli is a family-owned and operated business and sits in the center of downtown. It's known for its high food quality; great customer service; and its remarkable view of the busy city as folk scurry around town.

"There he is, my main man!" Exclaims Jay as he enters the deli door and approaches Tim.

Jay and Tim greet one another with a close embrace as they perform a lengthy, ritual handshake. Jay and Tim are more than best friends, they are also fraternity brothers.

As soon as the fellas sit down, Tim says, "So what did you do last night?"

Jay's face quickly tenses up as it dawns on him that he forgot to call Tim. Before Jay could respond, Tim interrupts him.

"You told me you were going to celebrate and you would call me if you did."

"I apologize,brother. I became a bit preoccupied."

With a look of disgust on his face, Tim asks, "Who is she?"

"Why does it have to be that I became preoccupied with a female?"

With his lips pushed outward mockingly and looking at Jay sideways, Tim replies, "Do I need to respond to your rhetorical question?"

"Ok, ok," replies Jay.

As Jay was about to share more about what he did last night, the waitress advances to the table. In a soft-spoken tone, she greets the men. "Good afternoon,gentlemen. May I start you all off with something to drink?"

Both men look up simultaneously. The waitress is a petite lady with snow-colored hair and glasses clinging to the bridge of her nose. She was sporting a white blouse with a black crossover tie, black pants, and a black waist apron with two pockets. Her oval-shaped name tag read Carolina.

Tim orders water with lemon and Jay orders water with no lemon.

"Great!" She replies. "I'll be right back with your drinks."

"Have you not heard?," Jay questions Tim.

"Heard what?"

"About the study where researchers found all types of bacteria on lemon wedges."

"No, but they also said that we shouldn't get our kids vaccinated either," replies Tim facetiously. "My grandmother used to say what won't kill, will cure."

"I'll remember that when I give your eulogy after you drink that tall glass of germs."

Both men laugh.

Sliding the glasses on the table, Carolina asks, "Have you all decided on what you're going to have today?"

Without hesitation, Jay orders the turkey club with extra mayonnaise and old-fashioned kettle potato chips. As Carolina turns her head in Tim's direction, she notices Tim strangely examining the glass of water.

"And for you,sir?"

"Ah – ah – I'll have the roast beef special and ah..."Tim pauses for a few moments. "Oh yes, and another glass of water! This time, without lemon,please. I'm sorry for any inconvenience caused."

"None at all,my dear. I'll have that out to you shortly along with your sandwiches."

"Ok, back to the young lady. Her name is Chantell, and she's a ten! Her conversation and her job are tens too! And her car..." Jay pauses for a second and says, "is a twelve! She seems too good to be true!"

Tim nods his head and replies cynically, "You never know. Things aren't always what they seem."

Immediately Jay's childlike exuberance left and his facial expression transforms from excitement to discontent.

"There you go again!" Jay replies petulantly. "Mr. I got hurt"so no one gets the benefit of the doubt. Besides, it was an accidental date, and I am not looking for anything longterm."

"Of course not," Tim replies. "I'm just noting that some-times people aren't who we think they are. That's all."

Carolina returns just in time to interrupt the conversation.

"Here's your order,young men. And here's your glass of water with no lemon!"

Both men thank her as Tim prepares to drink his bacteria-free water.

Jay realizes that he may have overreacted and quite possibly may have offended his friend who has every reason to be skeptical about relationships.

With a face swathed with shame, Jay replies, "You're right, and I'm sorry for being insensitive."

"It's cool. I'm just trying to look out for you like I'm sure you would do for me."

Jay and Tim finish their meal, as Jay prepares to return to work.

"Alright Tim, thanks for lunch. I have a very important meeting in thirty minutes."

"Is it more important than the very important meeting you had the other day?," Tim asks snidely.

Laughing as he walks away fastening the buttons on his suit jacket, Jay replies, "It most certainly is,my brother, it most certainly is!"

Later during the meeting, Jay was undoubtedly distracted. He couldn't get the images of Chantell out of his head. He was reminiscing about last night and how stunning Chantell looked. Then,Jay thought to himself; I wonder when she is going to call. The way she was looking at me last night, I know she's interested.

"Great job,Jay!" Yells Charles Reedy, the forty-something multi-millionaire Managing Director.

Jay is staring through the conference room window with a hollow expression and fails to acknowledge his praise.

Grasping both sides of his tailor-made suit, Mr. Reedy clears his throat and again congratulates Jay.

Snapping out of his temporary daydream, Jay replies, "I'm sorry."As you were saying..."

"Jay, you played a huge role in the success of this deal! You have been doing exceptional work consistently. As a matter of fact, why don't you come up here and receive this handsome token of appreciation."

Jay walks up to the front of the plush conference room to resounding applause magnified by the acoustics built into the room.

"Thank you so much!" Exclaims Jay.

"No, thank you, Jay," replies Mr. Reedy. "Keep up the good work. I see great things in your future." Mr. Reedy smiles while rubbing his fourteen-karat gold Managing Director's lapel pin.

As Jay is heading back to his seat, Mr. Reedy leans over to Jay's Senior Director and asks, "Is he okay. He's usually a little more exuberant when he receives his bonuses."

"Maybe it's extreme focus. Jay's been on a roll, and I'm sure he is anticipating becoming a Senior Director soon."

"You're probably right," replies Mr. Reedy nodding his head

in agreement.

Joseph Nixon

CHAPTER 3

A few days pass and no phone calls from either side. Jay then decides to give Chantell a call.

Chantell's cell phone rings as she and her best friend Cindy are on their way to have a girls' day out. Cindy is a married, conservative but high-powered defense attorney who lives with her husband on the outskirts of the city or as Chantell describes it, the country.

Chantell picks up her phone and realizes it is the Banker she met the other night but refuses to answer.

"Why aren't you answering your phone, Chantell?," asks Cindy. "You make way too much money to be avoiding bill collectors, so who are you trying to avoid?" Both women laugh boisterously. "Seriously, Chantell, what is his name this time?"

"I was almost offended. You made it seem as if I've been with so many guys," replies Chantell, as she looks directly at Cindy giving her the death stare.

"I didn't mean it that way," replies Cindy. "But I need you looking at the road and not at me."

Both women giggle.

"Well, it's some handsome accomplished guy I met the other night," Chantell replies.

"Well, answer the phone," cries Cindy.

"That's the thing. I don't want this guy to think that I am all that interested. Remember, I am not looking for any relationship."

"How do you know that he is looking for a relationship?"

"Because he looks like the type," laughs Chantell.

"Is it a bad thing to be in a committed relationship?"

"Yes, if you don't want to be in one! Who wants the stress of having to check in or call in their whereabouts or having to get permission or compromise or longing for validation?"

"Is that the way you view relationships?"

"Ah – yes!"

"Have you ever considered therapy?"

"Why would I be going to therapy? I am quite fine," yells Chantell.

As they arrive at their favorite spa, Cindy could sense that Chantell does not want to address the issue any further and wants to spend quality girl time, so she leaves it alone. The girls continue their day out and Cindy doesn't bring up the topic again.

"This chair is too relaxing," whispers Cindy as she sinks deeper into it. "What do you think?"

With closed eyes, Chantell responds in a low voice, "I think you should enjoy it and stop with all the questions,Katie."

"Katie – who's Katie?"

"You know Katie –Katie Couric!"

The women grabbed each other's hand as they look at one another giggling.

Cindy then replies, "I'm so fortunate to have such a great friend."

"Me too," replies Chantell.

The ladies continue their manicures and pedicures before heading home for the evening.

As Cindy opens the door to the foyer of her home, Todd,the kids, and two Pomeranian dogs greeted her with excitement. As the little ones compete to see who can climb up Cindy's leg the fastest, Todd asks his wife about her day.

"Did you all have a good time," asks Todd as he reaches for her designer purse.

"It was relaxing, and it is always nice to spend time with Chantell whenever our schedules permit."

"Oh, by the way, Chantell has this successful guy pursuing her,and it doesn't appear that she wants to pursue anything with him," shares Cindy.

"After you have experienced unsuccessful relationships where you have given the best of you and folks disappoint you each time, you become cynical. Do you blame Chantel," asks Todd.

"Of course not! I don't blame her,but I feel when she encounters the quote, unquote right person, she's going to miss out.

Maybe we can just invite her to church,and she can find a successful guy there that would appreciate her and treat her like the queen she is," says Cindy.

"Well, why didn't you think of that earlier babe,!Because every guy who attends church is a perfect person with no flaws – right?" asks Todd mockingly.

"Come on, babe, now you're just ridiculous."

"I'm just saying – trust is something that is hard to regain once it's lost. I think Chantell is having a difficult time trusting men. I think the best thing you can do is provide unconditional support to her and she will eventually figure it out."

"Thank you so much, Dr. Johnson! You know just what to say to make me feel better about a situation."

"Yeah, well wait until you see this dinner I prepared for you," said Todd.

CHAPTER 4

Two weeks after they met, Jay receives a phone call from Chantell.

"Hello, Mr. Banker, how have you been?"

"Very well," replies Jay.

Jay feels the urge to ask Chantell why she didn't answer his phone call, but he wants to play it cool as if he doesn't care.

"So, what have you been up to?," Jay asks.

"Just working hard and making families dreams come true."

"So, what are you doing this Friday night?," Jay asked hesitantly.

"I'm not sure. My girlfriend Cindy and I have plans to go out this Friday night. Why?"

"Oh, I was hoping that you and I could try out that fairly new Italian restaurant downtown and hopefully get to know each other a little better—but that's alright. If your plans with Cindy change, I would like you to give me a call. Anyway, I have a conference call with the sales team and traders in five minutes. It was nice hearing your voice again."

"Same here," replies Chantell.

As Jay hangs up the phone, he is smiling on the inside. He can't help thinking that Chantell seems to be playing hard to get but that's quite alright because she's fine enough for him to play the game too!

That Friday morning Jay surprises Chantell with a phone call.

"Good morning, beautiful," says Jay. "How are you this morning?"

"I'm doing fine," replies Chantell cautiously.

"I wanted to know if you were free for lunch today considering that you had dinner plans tonight."

"I would love to, but I have a few errands to run today."

"Oh well,that's fine," Jay replies. "I have a cluster of paperwork I need to complete. I'll just stay in the office and catch up."

Jay feels conflicted because he is a little disappointed, but he is unsure why.

Before Jay could even come to terms about his internal conflict, Chantell replies, "I am free tonight though! Cindy canceled. She had to accompany her husband to a gala this evening."

"Ok, so what time should I pick you up?," replies Jay excitedly.

Chantell pauses for a second before she responds. With all the stillness that followed, Jay thought that perhaps he came across too eager and was giving off the wrong impression. What was I thinking, Jay thought to himself. He doesn't want things to seem more than what they truly are.

Chantell then broke her brief silence and replies, "We just met,Mr. Banker! How about I meet you at the restaurant at seven o'clock?"

"Sounds good to me. I will send you a text with the address."

"Ok, I'll see you tonight," Chantell replies.

Jay sends a text message to Chantell with the address as he leaves work early to make sure he gets to the barber shop at a reasonable time. As Jay enters Men of Distinction, the most renowned barbershop in Atlanta, he is welcomed by the hostess Ms. Cheryl.

Ms. Cheryl is a middle-aged southern belle with a distinct southern drawl! She is charming, polite and always wears an enchanting smile on her face. She could pass for twenty-eight and looked like she never had a drink or smoke in her life. She always has flawless hair and makeup and her style was unique, especially her purses!

"Good afternoon, welcome to Men of Distinction, where a great haircut and a wonderful experience is what you deserve! Do you have an appointment?"

Jay smiles, as the hospitality here never gets old. "Yes, I most certainly do," replies Jay! "I called earlier – Jay Walker."

"Oh yes,Mr. Walker, I have you down for a four-thirty appointment. Please take a moment to look at the complimentary cocktail list and tell me what you would like as you await your appointment."

Jay had some idea of what he wanted to drink,but as Ms. Cheryl hands Jay the drink menu, her incredible fragrance abruptly befuddles him. "What was I going to order again?," Jay murmurs to himself. Jay skipped his usual Patron and chose something different, so he ordered the Ciroc Lola, which according to the menu consists of vodka, liquor, pomegranate juice, orchid, and champagne or as Jay likes to call it champan-ahh!

Jay was relaxing as he lounges in the waiting area watching the other businessmen network while playing a game of pool, chess or better yet reading a newspaper while enjoying a shoe shine.

It was now four twenty and Jay knows he must finish his drink because this barber shop prides itself on making good on their appointments – except Jay's Barber at times; who is a bit of a misfit or maybe renegade is a better word.

Nine minutes later, Cheryl hangs up the phone and says, "Mr. Walker, you are free to go back now. Enjoy your experience!"

Jay proceeds to the back of the barbershop. This barbershop is like no other barbershop. The dark brown wooden floors are glossy; all ten of the handcrafted barber chairs have hides of leather trimming, the headrests are made with foam with the name Men of Distinction masterfully embroidered into it. Flat screen TVs decorate the walls of each barber station playing sports and business stations, as do the spa rooms and bathrooms.

"What's up slick," Jay says with both hands raised.

"Besides all these heads up in here, child support, and rent for this seat…I could go on and on," replies Tyrone, Jay's Barber.

"I am doing the VIP thing today! How much is that again," Jay asks.

"Come on, brother, it's only sixty dollars."

"Sixty," Jay paused, "plus the twenty I usually tip," Jay paused a second time, "hmmm, that's eighty dollars!"

"I see the bank has been helping your math, replies Tyrone sarcastically. Here it is I am thinking that you got the position because of EOCC."

While laughing hysterically, Jay replies, "I see you got jokes and I think you meant the EEOC."

"Yeah, yeah, something like that."

"I like the variety added to the complimentary cocktail list, and the new bow tie look – I'm feeling that big time!"

"I will be sure to let the boss man know that you gave your stamp of approval," says Tyrone as they both chuckle.

"So, who is she?" asks Tyrone.

"Why does it have to be a female?"

"It doesn't have to be,brother. Your sexual preference is your sexual preference. You like what you like. I promise I won't judge you."

"Hold up man," replies Jay. "I didn't mean it like that."

"Oh, OK. You are asking for the works! Every time you do the VIP thing, it's about a date, and you're in a rush. You usually get the distinguished gentleman haircut and even after you're done, you sit while we debate sports and politics."

"Well, I met an extremely attractive young lady at Exquisite about two weeks ago."

"You mean that fancy jazz club for rich folk."

"Yes! She's a real estate agent and appears to have it to-gether."

"I find it interesting that you used the term appears," replies Tyrone as he places the barber cape around Jay's neck.

"Don't get me wrong,brother, I am not a huge skeptic, but we only had one accidental date."

Tyrone shut off the clippers and pulled them away from Jay's head.

"So,let me get this straight, you accidentally went on a date with a gorgeous woman that appears to have it all together,that you didn't plan?"

Before Jay could respond, Tyrone then responded, "So that's the trick! No wonder why I haven't been able to attract that special lady."

Jay then sits upright and asks, "Why is that?"

"Simple, I have been intentionally trying to date the right

women when all I have to do is bump into Mrs. Right on accident," Tyrone replies.

Jay and Tyrone both burst out into laughter. "You joke way too much! Besides, it's going to take a really special lady to be with me because of my share of flaws."

Tyrone leans back as if he was surprised at what Jay said and then states, "You are sure right, you are definitely flawed,my brother! Last time you came in here, you only tipped me ten dollars. For a "big timer" such as yourself,that's unacceptable!"

"Well, if you quit cracking jokes and get me out of here in a reasonable time, you just might end up with the usual tip."

"Ok, let me make sure you look like a million bucks for this date. I know exactly what you want. Not too low, with a temp fade on the sides and back, with no sideburns, right?"

"Absolutely," exclaims Jay.

"Oh, I almost forgot, would you like the baby face too?"

Jay wasn't paying much attention as he replied, "Yeah, I listen to Baby Face, why?"

"No dude, I meant are you keeping the goatee, or should I cut it all off?"

"Oh, my bad brother, I'm keeping the grown man look! I was thinking it was kind of strange for you to be asking me if I listened to Baby Face."

Jay and Tyrone laughed and laughed. The barbershop experience was the perfect prelude to Jay's date because it helped to alleviate some of the anxiety he was feeling.

Jay finishes up his haircut and heads home to prepare for his date.

Joseph Nixon

CHAPTER 5

Jay is pacing up and down his walk-in closet rummaging through his most sophisticated evening suits, debating what he will wear.

Meanwhile, Chantell is at home on her cell phone with Cindy.

"Hey girlfriend, are you excited about tonight?," asks Cindy.

"I am excited to see him again and to get to know him better but as we both know I am not looking for anything long-term."

"I think tonight you should ask him about relationships and his interests."

"I just want to have a good time tonight. I want to be spontaneous. I don't believe in prescribed dates."

"You do have a point there. Well, my only advice for you

tonight is to enjoy yourself and most importantly, be yourself."

"What does that supposed to mean!?" Chantell asked with a tone of annoyance.

"I'm sorry, replied Cindy in a contrite tone. All I'm saying is that people always meet your best you and when I say "you" I mean you as in all of us. When we meet people or are getting to know people, we introduce them to our representative. Our representative does an outstanding job of promoting the best of us. All I'm suggesting is that you be as comfortable as you can be on this date and if it ever materializes to anything in the future, there will be fewer surprises. Just make sure he meets the real you!"

"Who am I speaking to again –Iyalna?" replies Chantell with a castigating tone.

"Why would you say that?" Asks Cindy.

"Because you're starting to sound like you're going to Fix My Life. It's only our second date and may I remind you, the first date was merely an accident," says Chantell.

"I believe everything is for a purpose."

"Whatever! I must get going now. I don't want to be later than I am already."

Chantell is staring at herself in the mirror holding up an elegant dress against her chest. Hmmm, this one will do the trick, she thinks to herself. Then Chantell ponders whether she was a bit harsh with Cindy.

Chantell reflects on the last time she was harsh to Cindy. It was a few years ago when Cindy took on a highly publicized sexual assault case. Chantell was upset that her best friend would defend someone that had appeared to be so guilty in the court of public opinion. Cindy recollects the conversation they had; I told her it could blemish her career. Cindy was steadfast in her decision and took on the case. As much as I hate to say it, she was right then. She won the case. Let's hope she's wrong this time, Chantell thinks to herself as she grabs her keys and heads to the garage.

As Chantell prepares to exit her luxurious suburban home, Jay has arrived at restaurant Agostino. The valet takes possession of Jay's keys as the hostess greets him.

"Good evening Mr. Walker! Please follow me."

Jay takes his seat and patiently awaits Chantell's arrival.

About seven thirty, Jay notices the host escorting Chantell to their table. She is wearing a shapely, white evening dress that is knee length, with gold earrings and designer heels. Jay is blown away by how beautiful she looks! Jay ascends quickly to his feet to assist Chantell with her chair.

Chantell looks around the restaurant at the serene elegance as soon as she entered the low-ceilinged, softly lit dining room.

With a look of astonishment on her stunning face, Chantell then says to Jay, "Agostino! This place is nice, Mr. Banker!"As she takes her seat.

With a big ol' grin, Jay replies, "I'm ecstatic that you like it! I thought this place would be fitting for a second date. You see, the name Agostino is Italian for Majestic, which means having or showing impressive beauty or dignity. After our accidental date, I must say that I was impressed by you."

"Wow! I am flattered you put that much thought into this date. So, tell me, who is Jay really?"

"Well, my full name is Jay Walker and I am originally from Atlanta. I am a graduate of the great Bethune-Cookman University with a bachelor's degree in accounting, and I earned my master's degree from Harvard School of business. I am thirty-five years old, and of course, you know that I am a banker. I work for an investment bank, and I am the youngest executive at my place of work. Who are you?"

"I am Chantell Randall. I am originally from Virginia Beach, Virginia. I am a graduate of the University of Pennsylvania, which at the time, was the number one school in the country for real estate majors. So, I am an Ivy Leaguer as well. I work for the top real estate firm in the city, and I am the top agent. I moved to Atlanta a few years ago when I accepted this position."

Jay and Chantell were both enjoying their dinner and each other's company when Jay asked,

"Chantell, how could a beautiful and accomplished woman such as yourself be all alone the night I met you?"

Apprehensive on what question would follow, Chantell replies, "Simple! I am not involved with anyone and my girlfriend Cindy wasn't able to make it out that night. I can ask you the same thing."

Jay looked and smiled.

"I was supposed to meet my buddy Tim that night, but I got a little sidetracked."

Chantell gave a coy smile and replied, "Oh my, are you suggesting that I was a bit of a distraction!?"

"You most certainly are," Jay muttered while clearing his

throat. "I meant were."

Chantell and Jay both started to laugh.

"So, tell me, what do you enjoy doing in your spare time," asks Chantell.

"I am a very simple guy. I enjoy working out, cooking and accidentally stumbling into gorgeous real estate agents at jazz clubs. What about yourself?"

"That's cute. I cannot say that I do a whole lot either. I am a workaholic, and occasionally I will spend the night out on the town with my best friend."

As Chantell was sharing, Jay couldn't help his wandering eyes. She was flawless from head to toe!

"I see you also find time to keep up with the latest fashion trends."

With an adorable grin on her face, Chantell responded, "Is that your way of saying that you like my style?"

Jay replies, "I most certainly do,and if you saw the way everyone was staring at you when you emerged at the top of the marble staircase, I would say they do too!"

Chantell then looks Jay directly in the face and says, "I en-joyed this date, but I must get going."

"So did I," replies Jay.

Jay then motions to the waiter for the check. Chantell tries to pay for her portion of the dinner, but Jay wouldn't let her.

"Maybe next time I'll let you get the check," Jay says.

In a joking manner, Chantell uttered, "Who said anything about next time."

Jay and Chantell left the restaurant and headed their sepa-rate ways. Chantell was very impressed. The date turned out to be more than she had anticipated. Chantell couldn't wait to call Cindy.

"Hey girlfriend, are you still up?," asks Chantell.

With the sound of a frog in her throat, Cindy replies, "Not really."

"Oh, I had the greatest time," declares Chantell. I must tell you all about it!"

"I think you missed the part when I said I was asleep."

Chantell is so excited she disregarded the apparent agitation in Cindy's voice and responded, "I heard you,but I knew you would certainly want to hear what took place."

"Well, since I'm up now, tell me what happened."

"To begin with, we went to this first-rate restaurant. The food, the experience, everything about this place was first class! Then I found out from Mr. Banker that he chose that particular restaurant because of the meaning of its name."

"What was the name," Cindy asks?

"Agostino," exclaims Chantell.

"Ok, what's the significance?"

"It means having or showing impressive beauty or dignity."

"So, let me get this straight, you were wined and dined, and now you are having second thoughts about becoming committed?," asks Cindy.

"Excuse me, is that what you heard!?"

"Oh, my fault, I just thought your tone was different than earlier, and no one knows you better than I do."

Chantell then pauses for a second before she responds to Cindy. "Look, Cindy, I was just sharing with my best friend that I had an exceptionally nice time. That's all! I didn't call and ask if you wanted to accompany me to the bridal store! Let's not get ahead of ourselves. For the last time, I am not looking for a commitment!"

"Alright friend, I have to get some sleep. I am very pleased that you had such a great time. I will talk to you tomorrow… Goodnight."

"Goodnight," replies Chantel.

CHAPTER 6

The following Monday morning, Jay gets a call from Tim. "Hey stranger, how was your date the other night?"

"It was fantastic!"

"Oh, that's why you never bothered to call me to tell me about it."

"Come on, brother, cut me some slack. I have been extremely busy as of late. I am underwriting for this huge development company that wants to go public."

"It's fine; we just need to catch the big game tonight.

"Great," Jay replied! Let's do Buffalo Wild Wings."

"But their girls are fully dressed, and they wear jerseys," replied a disappointed Tim. "I was thinking the owl girls (Hooters) or Wing House.

"You do have a point there, but I like to hear the game too!"

Tim then replied, "Alright, only because I love you, brother."

Later that evening, Tim and Jay had a few drinks enjoying the game when Tim asked, "Does she know your situation?"

"What do you mean does she know my situation," replies Jay with a scowl on his face?

"You know…the situation."

"Look, I am here to watch the game, and as I said to you on several occasions, I am not looking for anything long term. So, my situation is irrelevant! Am I going to start to feel like I am on the Dr. Phil show during a Monday night football game?"

"No, no!" Replies Tim. "I was just asking because it seems like you are starting to enjoy her company and if that's the case,hopefully you would want her to know all about you up front just in case it goes anywhere."

"Tim, for the last time, I am not looking for that type of relationship, so my situation doesn't matter right now."

Tim and Jay continued to watch the game, and Jay's "situation" is never addressed again.

The next morning, Jay receives a call from Chantell.

"Hello,Mr. Banker. How are you?"

Chantell's voice seemed seductive, but Jay didn't want to read too much into anything.

"I'm better now that you called."

"Are you trying to make me blush?"

"That wasn't my intent. I was just trying to be honest."

Chantell then responded, "I enjoyed our date. I thought chivalry was dead, but you made me feel otherwise the other night."

"I'm glad you enjoyed yourself. You are interesting and fun."

"I was wondering if you would be interested in going out on a date of my choice," asks Chantell.

Internally Jay's response is hell yeah, absolutely but he has to play it cool.

"Sure, why not. If this date is as fun as the last, I say we'll have a really good time."

Chantell then arranged the third date for Friday night.

As Jay approaches the restaurant, he is anxious, wondering if their third date would go as well as the first two, even though one was an accident as they both coined it.

This place is quite fancy; Jay thinks to himself as he steps out of his car and gives his keys to the valet. As soon as Jay enters the door, he is greeted by the lead host.

"Name and reservations, please?," asks the lead host.

"Jay Walker,"

"Oh, so you are the incomparable Jay Walker!?"

Lost for words, Jay responds, "that will be me."

"I have been waiting for you, Mr. Walker. Well, right this way,sir."

As Jay approaches the table, again he's blown away by Chantell's beauty and her classiness.

"Hello, Mr. Banker. Welcome to J. Nix, the number one-rated restaurant in the city and the best-kept secret!"

Jay stopped and scanned the room. The decor was strikingly contemporary, with breathtaking views. The dining room consisted of all white chairs and tables with a huge crystal chandelier that hung in the center of the room, acting as a halo and creating a timeless romantic atmosphere. It was spectacular!

"I must say; I knew you had great taste, but this is extraordinary," Jay exclaimed.

The server approached the table dressed like a Buckingham Butler. However, he was wearing all white.

"What can I get the lovely couple to drink?"

Did he just say a couple? Jay thinks to himself. Do we look like a couple? Is that the impression we are giving off? Right before Jay could say anything, Chantell responded."Oh, no! We're just friends enjoying dinner."

Whew, that was close, Jay thinks to himself.

The server apologetically responded, "I'm sorry ma'am, sir. What would you lovely folks like to drink?"

"I'll have pink Moscato," replies Chantell.

"And I'll take Patron chilled, please."

After ordering their drinks and entrée, Chantell and Jay were relishing their time together. They learned a little more about each other's interests, but they never really touched on relationships. They walked away from their third date even more enthused than they were following their last date.

As they exited the restaurant, Jay looked at Chantell whose eyes were gleaming with innocence and said, "I had a great time!"

"I did too,Jay," replies Chantell.

Caught up in the moment, Jay replies, "Maybe we can do

this more often."

Chantell replies, "We'll see what happens," as she drives off.

Jay and Chantell go out on numerous dates over the next six months. They are savoring spending time together and are feeling comfortable with one another.

Chantell decides that she will call Cindy. "Hi Cindy, how are you?"

"I am great Chantell, how are you?"

"Cindy, Cindy, Cindy. I think I am ready to take the next step with Jay."

"Wait a minute! You mean to tell me you are considering a relationship with him?"

"Girl, no, I am physically attracted to Jay, and I would like to act on my attraction."

"You mean sex?"

"Oh, come on Cindy, of course, I mean sex."

"Don't you think that's going to complicate things?"

"Not if you are up front and explain that you don't have any interest in a long-term relationship, and you are just trying to meet your grown-up needs."

"You mean grown-up wants, right?"

"Listen, Mother Teresa, stop acting as if you were never single! I was thinking I could invite him over for dinner and see where it goes from there."

"Do you think that is safe," asks Cindy.

"Well...I didn't do a background check, so I am not quite sure," says Chantell snidely.

"Well just let me know how it goes."

"Either way, I am your best friend, and I will always have your back. Even when I think you're...never mind, just let me know how it goes."

Jay is on his way home from work when he receives a call from Chantell. Jay's face lights up before he could even answer the phone. In haste, Jay dropped his cell phone between the driver's seat and the armrest. Jay clambers to get his cell phone, squeezing his arm down the little opening before he misses the call.

"I got it," exclaims Jay. "Hi, hi beautiful, how was your day?," Jay mutters as he gasps for air.

"I had a pretty relaxed day, and I was able to go grocery shopping."

"Wait a minute; I thought the butler took care of that!"

"Oh, so you have jokes."

"I'm just kidding… or maybe I wasn't."

"I was wondering if you would like to join me for dinner tonight at my house."

"It depends on who is catering," replies Jay sarcastically.

"Look, funny guy, I'm a fantastic cook!" Chantell pauses momentarily and then replies, "When I decide to cook."

"Well say no more! I'll be there around seven."

"Seven works," replies Cindy.

As Jay approaches Chantell's gated community, a burly security guard greets him and then calls Chantell to confirm that she is expecting a visitor.

"Alright sir, I have confirmed that Ms. Randall is expecting you. You may proceed."

Jay enters the driveway, he's amazed at Chantell's French-inspired home. It was country elegance at its best. His mind starts to wander a bit, but he quickly snaps back to reality and walks to the door.

Chantell met Jay at the door and escorted him to the washroom so he could wash his hands before dinner. Jay sat down for dinner, and the conversation ensued.

"You have a gorgeous home," replies Jay.

"Why thank you. I think it's pretty modest compared to some homes in this community."

Modest, Jay thinks to himself. That's a huge understatement! This house is about eight thousand square feet and never-ending. The architectural design of the home is remarkable which includes a wine cellar, an amazing bar, an old fashion fireplace,and antique wooden floors. The home gives off the feel of a French castle or better yet, an upscale hotel. It is simply inspirational.

"Did you sell this house to yourself?," asked Jay.

Jay and Chantell both laughed.

"No. If I did, the house would have been a whole lot bigger because I am one heck of an agent!"

As they continue to chat and chew, Jay's mind is racing. Chantell has this facial expression that isforeign to him. I think she is thinking what I am thinking. Maybe that's why she invited me here. Jay ponders.

Chantell then gets up and walks over towards Jay and says, "You look stressed," as she massages his shoulders slowly.

Jay's eyes roll in the back of his head as he slouches further and further into the chair. This massage feels a whole lot better than my electric neck pillow; Jay thinks to himself. Jay eventually places his hand on top of Chantell's hand and rubs her hand hesitantly.

Jay just knew that he would get popped, but that was a chance he would take. After receiving no resistance, Jay continues to rub Chantell's hand when it happened. They locked lips and kissed each other passionately! Chantell pulled Jay towards the winding staircase as they continued to kiss each other. As Jay's wandering hands rubbed against Chantell's butt, he realizes this was premeditated! That made him more hyped all the way to the bedroom!

Just outside the bedroom door, Chantel,caught up in the moment, asks, "Wait a minute, wait a minute, what does this mean?"

Jay thinks to himself, how dare she interrupt this incredible moment with a question like that?

Jay replies, "I want what you want," as he picks Chantell up off her feet.

The bedroom door closes and the fireworks begin!

Immediately after, the pillow talk began.

With sweat dripping from her brow Chantell asks, "So where does this leave us?"

Jay felt the obligation to say what he thought Chantell wanted him to say,so he replied, "I guess this makes us official."

"What does that mean exactly?," asks Chantell.

"We have been spending significant time together lately, and I have enjoyed every moment of it. Our communication is great, and we share so many things in common."

Chantell agrees with Jay as they hold hands in bed.

After about thirty minutes of spooning, Jay asks, "Do you mind if I wash up now?"

"Of course not," responds Chantell blissfully.

As Chantell gets out of the bed to secure the items Jay

requested, Jay marvels at her figure. Wow! Jay thinks to himself. She is flawless and terrific in every phase of life. How can she be all by herself?

After getting himself together, Jay shared that he had to get going, and he wanted to thank Chantell for one of his best dining experiences to date.

With a huge smile on her face, Chantell responds, "One of the best!?"

CHAPTER 7

As Jay departs Chantell's driveway, he immediately wrestles with his thoughts about the date. He thought to himself...that was incredible! The dinner was good, but the desert was even better. Then Jay paused for a minute and pondered that he just agreed to a relationship with Chantell. A commitment was the very thing he wanted to avoid. Jay then gives Tim a call.

"Tim, guess what!?"

With a false sense of excitement, Tim replies, "You won the lottery!?"

"Stop with the sarcasm already! Can't you ever be serious?"

"I'm sorry,brother. What's going on?"

"Chantell and I took that step.

"What step?"

"We acted on the physical."

"Okay but we are not in high school anymore, and we do not always share when we act on the physical unless there is more."

"That's why I am calling you. I think we committed to something."

"It was the dreaded pillow talk," cried Tim. "Wait a minute... did you go in without being clear that you were not interested in a relationship?"

"We never really discussed relationships. I thought that I would have an opportunity to discuss the fact that I was not interested in commitment, but we were having so much fun that it never came up."

"So where do you go from here?," asks Tim.

"I'm not sure because you know my situation. I know I have

feelings towards Chantell,but my situation always helped me to keep relationships in perspective, but I slipped up this time."

"Well, look at it on the bright side, you haven't walked Chantell down the aisle yet, or are you calling me from a chapel in Las Vegas," asks Tim.

"Come on, brother. I really could use your advice here," cries Jay.

"It is still early in the game, and you still have the opportunity to make Chantell aware of what you have going on," replies Tim. You just have to be honest and share your situation."

"That sounds easier said than done but you're right. Look, man, thanks for always being supportive when I need someone."

"Anytime, Jay."

"Goodnight, brother."

"Goodnight, Jay."

The following morning Jay was feeling ambivalent about

his new relationship with Chantell. She's so well rounded and gorgeous to boot! Jay's also aware that his situation might not let him go where his heart is willing to take him.

While Jay is pondering his night, Chantell is eager to tell Cindy all about the dinner date. Chantell decides to text Cindy. The text read:

Good morning Cindy! Let's meet up for brunch later. I have to tell you what's going on with me! LOL

Cindy returned a text that read:

Smh (shaking my head)...I will definitelybe there! I like your talks; they always come with food, LOL.

Chantell and Cindy meet for brunch and Chantell shares last night experience with Cindy. Cindy had appeared to be excited for Chantell until she got to the part about commitment.

"Wait a minute,you told me that you were not looking for any commitment, what happened?"

"I'm not sure,but I think there's something special about Mr.

Banker."

"Did the two of you ever discuss relationships and commitment?"

"No, we didn't," Chantell replies.

"So, you are not even sure if he wants to be in a committed relationship or not? It could have just been pillow talk!"

"I am not sure about the pillow talk thing. I think it's more than that."

Chantell and Cindy finish up their brunch.

"Thank you for the meal,and I sure hope things work out for you. You are an incredible woman and deserve someone to treat you special."

"No problem friend...anytime."

As Chantell makes her way to her car,she receives a text from Jay. The text read:

Last night was great! Thanks for the dinner and the dessert was to die for! I will call you later when I get the chance, LOL.

Chantell responded:

Last night was great for me too," Ttyl (talk to you later)!

Later that afternoon, Jay called Chantell to thank her for such a wonderful time. Chantell shares she equally enjoyed their dinner experience and wants to reflect on their new commitment.

"So how does it feel to be official,Mr. Banker!?"

Jay was afraid that Chantell would broach this topic and he was more interested in discussing anything but that. Jay responded, "I think it is a good thing."

"Your response wasn't very convincing,Jay," replies Chantell in a disappointed tone.

"Well, that's not how I was trying to come off. I truly enjoyed spending time with you. "There's something that I wanted to talk to you about."

"That's strange because I have something I want to discuss with you as well," exclaims Chantell.

Jay has no idea what Chantell is about to say,but he desperately wants to make her aware of his situation before they go any further in this relationship.

Jay then replied, "You go first."

Chantell responded, "I was skeptical when it comes to guys because I am career driven and I hadn't experienced much success with relationships recently. I was content with taking care of my mature needs while maintaining focus on my life. Commitment takes work with the right person, and with the wrong person…good luck!"

Jay is starting to feel a bit uncomfortable because he is anxious as to where this soliloquy is heading.

"You make me feel special and unlike any other guy that I had ever dated."

Jay is now feeling nauseous because he enjoys Chantell's company too,but he is not ready to make the level of commitment she seems ready to make.

"I am flattered. You are pretty remarkable yourself," Jay uttered.

Feeling a little pressured, Jay decides not to share his situation or his true feelings. Jay does not want to hurt Chantell,so he just went along with the conversation.

CHAPTER 8

Time passes, and Jay and Chantell have been seeing each

other for more than a year. Everything appears to be fine be-

cause they have so much in common despite Jay's situation.

Chantell calls Cindy up. "Hey, girlfriend!

"Excuse me, who am I speaking with?"

"Oh, I see you are pretending to be a comedian today."

"It's been a while. Like a few weeks."

"I'm sorry, Cindy, but I wanted to discuss something with

you."

"What is it?," Cindy asks curiously.

"I am thinking about asking Jay to move in with me."

Cindy breaks out into coughing as if her drink went down

her windpipe.

"Are you serious?," replies Cindy.

"I am. Our relationship has been unbelievable,and we have been seeing each other for over a year now."

"That's a huge step,and you know how I feel about shacking up!"

Chantell then breaks out into a gospel song.

"Lord prepare me, to be a sanctuary, pure and holy, trite and true…"

"That's not funny, replies Cindy,and it's tried and true."

Chantell is laughing hysterically.

"Times have changed. I love this guy,and I want to spend the rest of my life with him. I can't do that if I am not sure whether or not I can live with him."

"I agree that people change, and you see more of who they are when you live with them. I still believe that you should be married before you live with someone. When you make that vow, you enter into a covenant to take the good with the bad,and therefore you should be able to work through whatever may come up."

In a real matter of fact way, Chantell responds, "I hear you, friend but marriage is supposed to be permanent and I want to be sure that I can at least live with Jay before I sign off on forever! Well, I am going to ask Jay out to dinner tonight,and I plan on discussing this then."

"Although I don't agree with this, I wish you the best, Chantell. I am praying for you."

"Thanks Cindy! Just make sure your heart is pure before you do that because I need for God to hear you."

"You always want to be funny Chantell."

"I love you, friend."

"I love you too."

Chantell calls Jay,and she is excited about setting up this date so she can ask Jay how he feels about moving in together.

"Hello, handsome!"

"Hi, gorgeous!"

"I had this really weird dream," replies Chantell.

Jay nervously replied, "Really, what was it about?"

"I dreamt that you wanted to take me to dinner tonight."

"Are you sure you were dreaming?"

"Yeah, I think so. I just thought I would make you aware since you have been making all of my dreams come true since I met you!"

Jay laughs hysterically. "Wow, was that your player line!"

Chantell laughs as well.

Jay then replies, "I will be more than happy to take you out tonight. I have some things on my mind that I need to share with you."

"That's perfect, exclaims Chantell because I do too!"

"I will be running late from work tonight, how about I meet you at Les Fontaines at seven thirty?"

"That sounds great!"

"Ok beautiful, I will see you later."

Jay then calls Tim.

"Hey Tim, how are you?"

"I'm good, brother. Are you okay? You don't sound like yourself."

"I plan on making Chantell aware of my situation. She is such a special lady,and I wasn't man enough to be honest and tell her how I felt about committed relationships nor did I share my situation with her. I was selfish. I didn't want to be disqualified too early before I even had a chance to hang out with her."

"You are doing the right thing because you have allowed the relationship to go too far. It is only fair that Chantell knows your situation. I wish you the best,and I want you to know that I have your back no matter what happens tonight."

"Thanks for being an incredible friend."

As soon as Jay hangs up the phone, he looks for an outfit;

our second date was much easier than going through my closet tonight, Jay thinks to himself. How could I be this selfish to
let this thing go so far, Jay thinks to himself. Jay then jumps
into his bed, which is big enough to fit the entire Brady Bunch
comfortably! Jay stares at his vaulted ceiling in disgust. He
looks over his right shoulder and notices that time has gotten
away from him some. It's seven o'clock!

Jay scurries out of the bed and back into the closet. It's all
or nothing. Jay gets dressed and heads out to dinner.

Jay arrives at the restaurant, his palms are moist,and the
uneasiness of what he is about to do was sickening. Jay
thought to himself, I better get it together! I care about her,so
I have todo what's right.

As Jay turns the corner of the restaurant, he notices Chantell. She couldn't have been any more beautiful than she was.

"Hi, handsome! Why do you look so distraught?"

"Oh, I'm fine."

Jay then motions to the waiter to get his attention and mimes,s'ilvous plait.

"Bonsoir, Monsieur, Mademoiselle," replies the waiter as he approaches the table. "How can I be of service to you?"

"I would like a glass of Bourgogne Chardonnay and a glass of pink Moscato for the belle femme!"

Chantell raises her eyebrow with a look of bewilderment and replied, "That's odd."

"What's wrong," Jay asks?

"I'm dumbfounded…you didn't order Patron."

She's right…Jay thinks to himself. That's all I ever order. Why did I order Chardonnay? I'm nervous. How is she going to take this?

Jay then replies, "I was trying to switch it up considering this is a French restaurant."

"Oh, ok," replies Chantell.

It doesn't appear that she's buying my explanation.

Chantell then reaches across the table and holds Jay's hands. She looks directly into his eyes and says, "So I have been thinking about our relationship and how much you mean to me. I have been at my best since we started spending time with one another. I feel like you complete me. Honestly, I had no intentions of being in a committed relationship when we first started hanging out,but after spending quality time with you, I fell in love with you, Mr. Banker. Seeing that we are so compatible, I was thinking that we should take the next step."

Wait a minute! Did my heart stop beating? Where is she going with this? This isn't fair,I still have to share my situation, Jay thought to himself.

"What next step?," Jay asked."

"I think we should move in together. That way we can see how compatible we are. My mother always told me if you wanted to know someone, go and live with them. I want to know you,Jay. I want to know if you are as special as a guy as you have made me feel for a little over a year now. You're such a gentleman and an intellectual,and I admire you so much for that."

Jay sat there dumbfounded not knowing exactly how to respond to Chantell.

Chantell then responded, "You are awfully quiet,Jay!"

"My bad, you've just been awfully talkative!" They both laughed.

Chantell then replied, "You see, you always know how to make me smile. What do you think about what I just said – you know, about moving in together?"

Jay then replied, "I think you need to let me share what I have before I respond to your question."

Chantell then sits perfectly upright, looking directly into Jay's eyes.

"I don't know how to say this but –" Jay pauses for an extended period of time."I am a registered sex offender," he says sheepishly.

Chantell's jaw drops and so does her glass of Moscato! Her face quickly transitions from blissful to despondent.

"What did you just say," asked Chantell.

In a low tone, Jay responded, "I am a registered sex offender."

"I can't believe this; I can't believe you!"

"Wait a minute, wait a minute, Jay cried! Let me explain. I was eighteen and went to a house party with my friends. I met this sixteen-year-old beautiful young lady, who told me she was seventeen. We were all partying and drinking. She tried some pills,but I didn't. We both got frisky and started kissing,and one thing led to another. We went up to one of the rooms upstairs and started having consensual sex. One of her male cousins at the party came to look for her and discovered us having sex in the room. She got scared that he would tell her parents and told me to stop. I stopped immediately,and she got dressed and left.

The next day, cops came to my house and asked me questions about the night before. They asked me if I knew the young lady and they also wanted to know were we drinking and using drugs. I told them I met her at the party. The cops asked me if I saw the young lady take any pills. I replied yes. They then questioned whether I took any pills and I responded no. They then arrested me and charged me with engaging in a sexual act with another by rendering unconscious or involuntarily drugging the victim.

It was some bull! Her parents had money,and we were not that well off. I had a public defender representing me. I was sentenced to a juvenile sex offender program,and I was required to registeras a sex offender. I promise you I did not do such a thing!"

Chantell is still astounded! "I have no idea what to say! I don't know if you are the man that I fell in love with. Why would you hold this information from me for so long? Who the hell are you!?"

"I'm Mr. Banker. I am the same guy you first met,and the guy that you said made you feel so special."

"No, Jay. That's who you wanted me to believe you were. This is a huge part of who you are. Are there any other surprises that you have not revealed, or have I finally met the real you!?"

THE DISCUSSION

INTRODUCTION

One of the biggest issues facing our society today is failing relationships. When I say relationships, I mean friendships, courtships and even worse, marriages. Now That I've Met the Real You is a book based on the premise that most of us struggle with being our "true" selves when we meet people for the first time, especially when we're trying to establish relationships. In my opinion, this is not a self-esteem issue but a lack of familiarity with a person. We're not sure what is considered acceptable and unacceptable behavior to that person, so we try to represent ourselves to the best of our abilities.

Sometimes people suffer from our intentional or unintentional lie. In other words, people meet our representative. Our representative replaces who we truly are because we're afraid. We're afraid of rejection. We're afraid that if we put our true person to the forefront, the person we are interested in establishing a relationship with will reject us.

I can remember my wife television surfing one Sunday evening looking for something interesting to watch when she stumbled upon Oprah Winfrey's "Super Soul Sunday" featuring Brene Brown. Oprah was interviewing Brene Brown about her book entitled Daring Greatly: How the Courage to Be Vulnerable Transforms the Way We Live, Love, Parent, and Lead. I immediately found myself glued to the TV screen when Brene was discussing the "Ted Talk" and her presentation on the power of vulnerability.

I was greatly intrigued because Daring Greatly or the ability to be vulnerable is the cure for many issues causing our relationships to fail. In Daring Greatly Brene Brown writes, "Connection is why we're here; it is what gives purpose and meaning to our lives. The power that connection holds in our lives was confirmed when the main concern about connection emerged as the fear of disconnection; the fear that something we have done or failed to do, something about who we are or where we come from, has made us unlovable and unworthy of connection." That's it! Our need for connection and the fear of rejection causes us to present who we are carefully.

I believe that if we are more honest with people at the beginning of relationships and offer more of who we truly are, we give people a reasonable opportunity to make an informed decision on whether they want to be in a relationship with us. We will be establishing a relationship with real authenticity. If they chose not to be in a relationship with us because of who we truly are, then we do not allow that to define who or what we are. That shouldn't affect our self-esteem or self-worth. All it means is that we're incompatible.

Imagine sharing your deepest and darkest secret with a stranger or better yet waking up naked lying next to someone you do not know. That's a pretty dramatic way of portraying falsehoods in relationships, but there are people out there who feel as if they have woken up to strangers and the people they thought they knew and love didn't exist. They are left with feelings of betrayal and hurt. They feel like they have been bamboozled!

Well, what's next? Once you discover that your friend or your spouse is not who you thought they were or portrayed themselves to be, what do you do next? Do you leave, or do you stay? Do you have enough love or history between the two of you to sustain that relationship or is meeting the real them, too much to handle?

MEETING THE
REPRESENTATIVE

"Relationships, easy to get into, hard to maintain. Why

are they so hard to maintain? Because it's hard to keep

up the lie!'Cause you can't get nobody being you! You

got to lie to get somebody! You can't get nobody look-

ing like you look, acting like you act, sounding like you

sound! When you meet somebody for the first time, you

are not meeting them. You are meeting their representa-

tive!" – Chris Rock, Bigger and Blacker (HBO, 1999)

Even the great Chris Rock believes that people find it difficult to reveal their "true" selves in relationships. Chris Rock understands that day after day we put up a front or do things outside of our character to persuade someone to be with us. One may ask, why do we do it? Well, in an Online article entitled Stop Pretending to Be Someone Else, author Jerry Kennedy posed that same question. Jerry thinks it's because we're afraid. Afraid of what other people will think, afraid that we might be wrong, afraid nobody will like us if we let them know who we really are.

We all know the experience of meeting someone for the first time. We get our best haircut or visit the salon; we wear our best clothes and spray on our best fragrances. We want everyone to remember us. We want to make a splash! That's fine if you always look jazzy and your hair is always intact but you and I both know that even celebrities except for Beyoncé didn't wake up like that, red carpet ready!

I liken the "representative" or the "poser" in relationships to an attorney-client relationship. We hire someone that goes before the court of law and presents our best case. In a myriad of situations, we never have to speak or take the stand to be cross-examined. Also, sometimes, we don't even have to show up in the courtroom. Our attorney's job is to represent our best interest and make us look good.

If we're honest, if most of us had to represent ourselves in a court of law, we would probably earn a thirty-year sentence for jaywalking! That's how horrendous we would be if we had to present our case before the court. At times, we believe if we present the "real us?, We would be looked upon by others in a similar fashion. Knowing that, we have consciously or subconsciously hired our best self to represent us when we engage in new relationships.

In 2009, Columbia Pictures released a romantic comedy entitled "The Ugly Truth," whereby Abby Richter, a morning show producer, played by Katherine Heigl is having the most challenging time dating and then finds some success when she teams up with Mike Chadway, a chauvinistic TV personality played by Gerard Butler. Abby reluctantly allows Mike Chadway to coach her on her quest to establish a relationship.

Initially, Abby experiences some success by utilizing persuasive tactics to lure the doctor she wanted a relationship with when Abby discovers the "ugly truth," which is she cannot continue to pretend to be someone she's not.

Despite the dysfunction that comes with pretending to be someone we're not, many of us continue to engage in misleading behaviors while establishing relationships. In Daring Greatly, Brene Brown writes, "...true belonging only happens when we present our authentic, imperfect selves to the world, our sense of belonging can never be greater than our level of self-acceptance."

Some of us have not truly discovered who we are. These are the folks you hear asking the question, "What does it mean exactly to be myself?" If you can't answer that question, then you have no business embarking upon a relationship anyway. You may inadvertently or like I suggested earlier in this chapter, unconsciously put your representative to the forefront and fail to give your prospective partner or friend an honest look at who you truly are.

In the article Stop Pretending to Be Someone Else, Jerry Kennedy suggests that while we are pretending to be someone else "...we're slowly dying inside. Keep turning off those aspects of your personality that you fear, one by one, and eventually you'll wake up one day wondering who you are and what you've done with your life. Trust me when I tell you that it's not fun. Fruitful and necessary, yes, but not fun. Because it's at that point that you have to start untangling yourself from the story and sorting out which bits are the real you and which bits were the version of you that was engineered to please others."

What many of us forget, is that sustainable relationships are built on trust. Having our representative go before us leaves room for trust to be broken in the future. Trust is supposed to be the basis for which we create an innocuous place for establishing authentic relationships. Trust is where true intimacy takes place.

When we are trying to forge relationships, we are supposed to be revealing ourselves to the people we are attempting to establish trust with. This will allow you to see if that person can handle our flaws, likes,and dislikes. Trust takes time,but it will allow you to feel safe in revealing who you are and whether that relationship is for you.

I know it may be difficult to be truthful because we have all unconsciously developed a characteristic that discourages us from putting our true person to the forefront, but I am encouraging you to "just be yourself!" Give people the honest opportunity to want to be in a relationship with you because of who you truly are. I believe there will be less surprises, healthier relationships and most importantly, they would have met the real you!

Joseph Nixon

THE CHASE

"Like a kitten chasing a string abandoned as uninteresting lifeless lint when you stop making it move, there are people, male and female, who prefer the thrill of the chase to the actual consummation of any kind of relationship. Unfortunately, you can't know who they are until they, too, stop playing with you and abandon the game and you with it like so much lifeless lint. No more dangling dancing string, no more incipient romance. Perhaps he or she has gone on to chase a livelier mouse, but you'll never know because they rarely stop to com-

municate."This excerpt was taken from an article entitled

The Thrill of the Chase? Published on May 14, 2010, by

Isadora Alman, MFT in Sex & Sociability

In more layman's terms, we have all pursued something that we thought we really wanted and when we attained it, we discovered that it wasn't all that we thought it would be. Maybe it had just lost its luster! Maybe it looked better on the rack or more enticing on the poster. Perhaps he or she appeared to be more interesting and compatible.

After you've met the representative, you experience the exhilarating period pre-relationship known as "the chase!" You find the representative physically attractive or intellectually interesting if you are not too shallow, and you have the desire to pursue that individual further. During the chase, you never really know what people's true intentions are. They could recognize something about you they like on the surface and might be interested in building upon that. Then,others like what they see and their end game is to conquer! It's almost as if dating is a "game of chance" where we have no influence over the outcome.

Joy Browne, the author of Dating for Dummies, was quoted saying, "In its purest form, dating is auditioning for mating (and auditioning means we may or may not get the part)." That may not seem like a very profound quote, but it is. An audition is a sample performance by a performer. During auditions, performers must be mindful that many people may have per-formed ahead of them. Therefore, when someone auditions for a part, they want to be at their best. Being at their best includes a lot of preparation but nothing is more important than "getting into character"

I am not a movie buff, but I know I've heard many famous movie stars say, the biggest thing to do to become successful is the art of "getting into character." "Getting into character" means you lose most of who you are to assume whatever persona the "character" you are portraying is supposed to be.

During the chase, we are in full character or simply, your representative is on top of the game! We are prepared to give a sample performance. We are fully aware that there were men and women who performed ahead of us; therefore, we must be on our "A" game! We want that part; we want to secure that role. "We're putting our best foot forward!"

What makes it so easy for people to unconsciously or consciously pretend to be something they're not during the chase? Like I said in the introduction, people aren't quite sure what is considered acceptable and unacceptable behavior when establishing relationships. They figure if they are at their best, then they have a greater chance of forging that relationship. What we don't consider during the chase is the amount of energy that it will take to sustain whatever does not come natural to us.

Guys that have never opened car doors for their moms are now in a full sprint to open the car door for the new lady in their lives. Now, now – don't get what I am saying misconstrued. I am not suggesting that guys shouldn't open car doors for their ladies because they didn't have practice in the past because progress is a beautiful thing. What I am suggesting here is, things that are not habits are much easier to stop doing. Eventually, our representative will get fatigued. Eventually, our representative will get frustrated. Eventually, our conscience will bother most of us and we will have to"give up the ghost!"

Interestingly enough, there are times when feelings are mutual during the chase and somehow, we neglect to discuss them because the chase has rules!

Yes, I said it! Don't act like you don't know the rules. I need not put them in any particular order but here are a few: Impress at all cost; don't appear to be too interested; offend no one; don't be the first to initiate contact and last but not least, you must go out on so many dates before you broach the topic of sex, well not so much anymore with sex.

These rules are unspoken but we know they exist and sometimes we honor them too much or not enough! When Jay and Chantell met, they both found each other attractive but they also knew that they were not looking for a committed relationship. The first date wasn't planned but on the dates that followed, maybe they should have discussed what they honestly thought about relationships. That's when they could have fought back their representative and based on where they were in their lives, shared that committed relationship was not something that they wanted to pursue. Then someone may have raised the question about meeting their physical needs. If they were both honest enough, they would have discovered that their feelings toward relationships were mutual.

We must remember, the chase is the most thrilling stage in dating but also the stage when we develop feelings from lust to like and possibly even like to love. We want someone to fall for

who we are and not who we are pretending to be. Talk about

what you like and dislike; be funny if you are funny; if you are

goofy, be goofy; but most importantly, have a blast being you!

Have a good time. If you are courageous enough to be au-

thentically YOU, then someone will be establishing feelings for

you based on YOU, and I think you just might be able to live

up to being you!

Joseph Nixon

PILLOW TALK

For some strange reason, men and women alike think the best time to discuss their true feelings for one another is during pillow talk. I describe pillow talk as any intimate conversation held right before you are about to engage in sex, during sex or immediately following sex. I think pillow talk is the most inopportune time to discuss feelings and can be very misleading. Men and women engage in pillow talk knowing that more often than not, answers are going to be flawed, yet they don't mind if the response is favorable.

Being transparent, I can tell you my wife used to believe the only time I would communicate is when we're in the bed and I was looking for sex. I can't say she is right in her assumption, but I can definitely say she believes she has my undivided attention. Most questions asked may very well get a favorable response. Who wants to answer the question wrong and "ruin the mood?" You see, Al Greene just sung "love and happiness," Marvin Gaye told us to "let's get it on," and Ella Mai is singing 'everything!" Sometimes women, but especially men, will do anything to keep the groove going.

I know you may have just raised your eyebrow but before you even go there, don't judge me! I am not alone. I am trying to help some of the brothers and sisters out there. Please, please, don't ask your man, lady, guy friend, boo, fiancé, wife, or husband anything important right before, during, or after sex! If you want an answer just to be able to say, "Remember you said," then that's fine. More than likely the response you will receive will not be authentic.

Although the story is fictitious, Chantell made a huge mistake when she asked Jay, "What does this mean?" Jay was aroused and ready! What else was he supposed to say? Jay found Chantell to be incredibly attractive since the night he met her, and he was awaiting this opportunity. Immediately following the act, Chantell wanted Jay to explain what he meant further, and he said that they were official.

In writing this book, I've seen many articles where people have suggested that pillow talk is one of the most effective ways of communicating in relationships. I suggested earlier that pillow talk can be misleading. I said that because we are vulnerable during pillow talk due to the stimulation and excitement involved. There are probably times when pillow talk can be open and honest. Also, sometimes, people feel comfortable sharing personal feelings but for the most part,it should not be a primary way of communicating in a relationship.

In an article entitled, What Happened to Courtship and Pillow Talk? The Loss of Romantic Sexuality, Randi Gunther, Ph.D. describes pillow talk as "The experience that follows orgasmic release is an intertwined state of wonderment, satiation, and openness. The partners are beautiful to each other. Like children in a state of bliss, they are able to share their most vulnerable fantasies and their deepest fears. Not wanting to feel the inevitable separateness of quieted arousal, they reach to one another in a different way, searching for new understanding and deeper connection."

Wow! Wasn't that intense!? That's the type of emotions that surround pillow talk and the reason I suggested avoiding asking questions that are near and dear to you. Avoid asking questions you intend to use to legitimize your feelings. Avoid asking questions you really want an authentic response to. If not, you just might get a favorable response to keep the groove going!

SHACKING UP

When I thought about the chapters I wanted to discuss in this book, I always knew this chapter would be the most intriguing and would stir up the most debate. Some of you all haven't even read the entire book to this point. You've probably skimmed through the book and I hope you are not disappointed.

There can be many factors that play into whether people should shack up but I gather from most people that shacking' up is a trial period for true compatibility.

Growing up, I've often heard my mother use the expression, "If you really want to know someone, go and live with them!" My mother was teaching us a profound life lesson I don't think we understood fully. My mother was trying to tell us that relationships change when you live with people. She was warning us about unauthentic relationships.

Partners attempt to validate shacking up by treating it as a trial period for true compatibility. Many people today would suggest that they want to be sure that they can live with someone successfully before they take bigger steps in their relationship such as marriage. It is easier and less nerve-wracking to move in together rather than making the commitment of marriage.

In the story, Chantell tells Cindy she wanted to see if she could live with Jay before she signed off on forever. Again, Chantell was treating that particular stage of her relationship like an "as seen on TV" infomercial. You can try this product for so many days and if you don't like it, you can return it and get your get your money back.

In an article entitled, "Shacking Up, How to avoid some potential pitfalls of moving in with your partner Samantha Joel, Ph.D. writes, "it's important to recognize moving in together for the investment that it is. A lot of couples move in together to try to "test drive" their relationship, figuring that if it doesn't work, they can just move back out. But moving in together isn't really a test — it's the real thing and moving back out may not be as easy as you expect. So, if you are not totally committed to your partner yet, it's important to realize that and to plan accordingly. That way, if and when you do decide to fully commit to your partner, it'll be because your relationship is fantastic, and not because you have joint custody of some furniture."

That was extremely insightful! As I stated earlier, many people shack up to assess true compatibility but sometimes during this phase in the relationship, other factors can cause them to continue to live together whether they are truly compatible or not. These factors can cause them to further validate the need for shacking' up.

Samantha Joel can be paraphrased stating that your commitment to your partner should be authentic and not because you all have joint custody of furniture. Furniture is one example but there are other examples that lead us further into relationships such as pets, assets and perhaps children. These are all possibilities of shacking' up and these factors can significantly influence whether people continue to shack up despite how they feel about their relationship.

The folks who claim they are shacking' up on a trial basis are hoping that things go well. They are not looking to "get their money back!",There are other factors that give us the feeling we have to continue to shack up despite our level of commitment.

When you live with someone, you get to see them at their best and when they are not so good. You get to see them with makeup and without makeup. Does he leave the seat up in the bathroom!? Were all of those meals just to get you to hook up because she or he doesn't enjoy cooking?

My mom was telling my siblings and me that shacking up will allow you to see people for who they truly are. It's easy to see someone occasionally for dates and maintain the facade of "Mr. or Mrs. Right." When you see someone daily, you get to experience all of their idiosyncrasies. I am not certain how often I patted my head when I dated my wife, but she hates it. She also hates the noise associated with me gnawing on my flesh after I have already eaten my fingernails and the skin surrounding it. Don't judge me!

The reason I mentioned my idiosyncrasies is very important. Those little unusual habits can be "deal breakers" as my buddy and I coined it, or just annoying. I am sure in the dating process I made a valiant effort not to succumb to some of my idiosyncrasies that I am so free to display in my marriage.

Aside from habits, there are other issues that can become more apparent as the representative starts to fizzle out. Effective communication may fade as poor communication emerges. It may become more difficult to get in the mood to totally enjoy sex because of some of the newly discovered issues.

I know a host of people who attribute some of their relational issues with "outgrowing their spouses." I will contend that we never really outgrow our spouse. It is my belief that the representative can be so great at times that we can be led to believe that we were actually on the same level.

We must remember, the whole idea about the representative is based on people being truly trying to forge a relationship and will do whatever it takes to make that happen. They are not sure what you will accept, so they will go the extra mile until they get what they want. Even if it means pretending to be on the same level or being nicer than they truly are. There is an end game but the harsh reality is we are oblivious to what their end game is. Fortunately or unfortunately, shacking' up will eventually expose their game.

Remember, shacking up is a commitment more so than it is a trial period or test drive. If you and someone you're dating decide to shack up, it should be treated as a major step in your relationship. Just be mindful there will be some surprises and other factors that will make it difficult to leave if you determine that the representative is not who he or she cracked up to be.

Joseph Nixon

HELLO STRANGER

I am sure most of you by now are familiar with the phrase "catfished!" The term catfish is used to describe people who meet Online and develop relationships only to find out that they have been deceived and their spouse turns out to be something other than they portrayed.

MTV even created a show called "Catfish" in which the father of the term, Nev Schulman, helps innocent folks realize that they are a part of a hoax.

Former Notre Dame football star and NFL linebacker Manti Te'o gave "cat fishing" a national platform as his phony relationship became the topic of sports debate on ESPN's "First Take" and Sports Center. Due to the extreme criticism surrounding the matter, Manti Te'o also had a sit down with at that time, queen of daytime Katie Couric. Manti Te'o experience displayed naïviety but more importantly, hurt and shame.

In context with the premise of this book, I think that it is far more damaging when the representative is exposed and you are introduced to the "stranger" than being "catfished!" You have spent time with the representative; made love to the representative; shared intimate feelings with the representative; and sometimes, moved in with the representative, only to discover that you have been deceived.

The representative wasn't a profile picture and someone you haven't physically seen. This is your soul mate, your fiancé and sometimes, your husband or wife. This is the point in the relationship when we ask ourselves, "where did this fool come from!?" In most cases we are really referring to ourselves. We are finding it difficult to believe that we have been bamboozled! This is also the point in the relationship when we have 20/20 hindsight and pinpoint the signs we missed.

You are mostly still shocked and in disbelief. "I can't believe he didn't open the car door!" "I can't believe he is speaking to me in that way!" "Her sex drive was through the roof and now, her back hurts all the time!" "I haven't had a cooked meal in days." "How long is the trash going to sit there?" "Is that his underwear on the floor in the bathroom?" It's like it happened overnight or with the snap of the fingers. It's as if the man or woman we fell in love with no longer exists.

This is the stage in the relationship when we question ourselves. We ask ourselves questions as if some revelation will drop from the ceiling! "What's wrong with me?" "Why didn't I see this coming?"

The answers are simple. He or she had one heck of a representative but as I've stated often in this book, the representative can become fatigued. The representative has a "shelf date." It can only last so long before it is no good, and then it expires. It's not your fault or his/her representative's fault. We're all guilty. Bishop Derek Triplett, former Pastor of Hope Fellowship Church in Daytona Beach, FL,and relationship coach, once said, "We need to teach people how to date to avoid playing games." We need to teach people to be authentic in the dating process. We must be ourselves, say what we like and dislike. Resist the temptation of the representative speaking for us.

That may seem trivial but it's the step toward "dating right," Remember the representative has a shelf life and will expire probably before you are expecting it to, therefore you will probably not be prepared for the lie or the convenient omission. The idiosyncrasies may rear their ugly heads and you may be left like Chantell with a broken glass and a drop jaw, staring in the face of a stranger asking yourself, "have I finally met the

real you!?"

Now That I've Met The Real You!

Gotcha! The representative has been exposed and now we've finally met the real you! "The real you" is angry, messy, mean, obnoxious, lazy, too ambitious, a liar, a cheat, too passive, a pushover and a host of other things we didn't think you would turn out to be. Okay, so now what!? You still have all these feelings and mixed emotions. What do you do with them? It's at this point in your relationship where all the so-called experts, such as your best friends and family members compete to determine who was the first to say, I told you so!

You have some tough decisions to make, especially if you shared personal stories, sacrificed yourself for others, share assets, made it to marriage or have kids. You now know the "situation!" You may experience a sense of uncertainty not knowing what your next move or moves should be. Then there's the feeling of disappointment knowing that your spouse or buddy turned out to be a fraud. These symptoms are all a sign of emotional discomfort. The pain you feel when a relationship has ended, or you think it should end.

What about the history? What about the kids? Like Samantha Joel pointed out, what about the furniture? Usually, when we unveil the representatives or the "posers" in our lives, we usually have some attachment, whether it's emotional or physical, that we must consider before deciding to leave or to stay. These are very important factors that even the most brilliant among us struggle to overcome.

I have a good friend I talk to all the time. We discuss a

myriad of issues and relationships is one topic that we discuss. Like Liz Lemon from the TV show 30 Rock, we've had multiple conversations about "deal breakers," which is any situation you consider too much for the relationship to continue. Different people have different levels of tolerances, and each relationship is unique. Once the representative tires out and the situation has been exposed, you must determine if that situation is a deal breaker or does the relationship mean more to you than the situation.

Dealing with the representative is the predicament that many of us and the people we know and love find themselves in too often. Most situations we face will not have a good ending or a right or wrong answer. Creating authentic relationships is the reason I wrote this book and the reason people need to meet the "real you."

There are so many residual effects of perpetrating the fraud in relationships. People are left with broken hearts and lose trust in others, kids end up in broken homes and left wondering what happened, friendships become cantankerous and impossible to maintain, all because we have been too afraid. We have been afraid to be who we are, to have people accept us for what we are. We have masked our identities and robbed people of authentic relationships.

Stop pretending to be something you are not. Be bold enough to be what you were intended to be and you will finally experience true intimacy in your relationships.

I want to end this book with a pledge I wrote entitled, "The Real Me!" I would like you to repeat this pledge every time you feel the need to have the representative replace the real you.

I am proud of who I am,

All of my habits make me unique,

I can trust my personality,

My personality makes me, me,

Anyone entering my circle,

Will be amazed by what they see,

But if there's one thing they'll never forget,

I will not sacrifice the real me!

ENDORSEMENTS

"Now That I've Metthe Real You is a must read for anyone looking for keys to understanding the roller coaster ride of relationships. Joseph Nixon provides the blueprint for taking off the mask we present when we meet people and arrive at a place of authenticity. This book is a fictional tale with real-world implications that will inspire you to live a more meaningful life." – Willie F. Williams, Community Leader and Proud Principal of Westside Elementary, Daytona Beach, Florida

Now That I've Met the Real You serves as a timely, relevant and current book. It is a direct approach to dealing with the elements of false relationships and humanistic behavior. It contains relationship lessons which include self-awareness, self- examination,and accountability. Its valuable lessons also educate us on recognizing the challenges that are prevalent in relationships while proactively preparing us to combat situations that are inevitable. Moreover, it allows us to create and foster an environment as well as relationships that are conducive to transparency and healthiness.

By reading this book, it will encourage couples to reveal their true self and intentions upon entering a relationship, in hopes of diverting unnecessary issues that are encountered as a result of creating false personas.

Dr. Chester Wilson, CW Consulting Firm, Doctor of Education Ed.D.